"A powerful allegory, Mr. Arkin's story can also be appreciated as pure entertainment. Suspense is generated in the opening chapter and maintained throughout. An unusual and memorable story."
— *Publishers Weekly*

"Look out conformity, here comes free will . . . He has brought it off efficiently and affectingly."
— *The New York Times*

"Arkin's brief book shares with the best of them a directness of telling and a sensitivity to the conflicting needs of the human spirit . . . There is a message here for the lemming in all of us."
— *School Library Journal*

"A winner."
— *Kirkus Reviews*

"A young audience will find meaning and interest in this beautifully written nature parable."
— *Horn Book Magazine*

THE LEMMING CONDITION

By Alan Arkin, the distinguished actor, producer and film director, and author of *Tony's Hard Work Day.*

the Lemming Condition

Condition

by Alan Arkin

Illustrated by Joan Sandin

A BANTAM SKYLARK BOOK

RLI: $\dfrac{\text{VLM 3 (VLR 3-5)}}{\text{IL 4+}}$

THE LEMMING CONDITION
*A Bantam Skylark Book / published by arrangement with
Harper & Row, Publishers, Inc.*

PRINTING HISTORY
*Harper & Row edition published April 1976
Bantam edition / September 1977*

ISBN 0-553-15016-2

Published simultaneously in the United States and Canada

*Bantam Books are published by Bantam Books, Inc. Its trade-
mark, consisting of the words "Bantam Books" and the por-
trayal of a bantam, is registered in the United States Patent
Office and in other countries. Marca Registrada. Bantam
Books, Inc., 666 Fifth Avenue, New York, New York 10019.*

PRINTED IN THE UNITED STATES OF AMERICA

0 9 8 7 6 5 4 3 2

To my mother and father

1

Sunlight streamed into the burrow, landed on the floor, worked its way slowly up the wall, and came to rest on Bubber's face. As it touched him Bubber woke with a start. He sat up, full of anticipation and ready to go. There was something important he had to do on this day, but what it was he couldn't remember. Nothing came to him. Bubber's sister, Sarah, was in the far corner of the room, sorting piles of clothing, and stacking the notes that she was forever taking.

"What's today?" Bubber asked urgently, blinking in the bright light. "What's going on today?"

Sarah stopped what she was doing and sighed a deep theatrical sigh, letting her brother know what a burden he was to her.

"Come on, for God's sake," said Bubber.

"Just tell me. Don't make a scene out of every-thing."

Sarah smiled at him as if he were an idiot and slowly made a long arc with her arm.

"Oh yes," said Bubber. He slapped his forehead with his paw.

"Have you got it?" asked Sarah.

"I've got it," said Bubber, and jumped out of bed.

"You won't forget now," said Sarah sarcastically.

"I won't forget," said Bubber.

He shook himself awake and went into the living room, ready for action. His parents, up for an hour, were radiating excitement: tidying things and making preparations. There was great random purpose to their activity. His father was stacking things in order, stepping back to get his bearings; his mother cleaning and dusting, setting things down, then dusting the same items over again. They were talking softly and intensely to each other.

"Ah! Bubber! Bubber!" said his father, raising an arm in greeting. He kept his arm raised as if he wanted to continue, but long practice at having nothing to say to his son left him paralyzed in salute.

"Can I help get things organized?" Bubber asked, wondering how long his father's arm would stay up.

"No, no, we've just about hrenhh . . ." he drifted off, unable to find the word, and moved a pile of magazines to where they had been five minutes before.

Bubber's mother was now talking quietly to herself, a longtime habit. She was telling herself exactly what she was about to do next. Bubber hated to interrupt her; her orders to herself seemed so terribly urgent. So he made himself a quick breakfast and started to leave the burrow with a long sack in his paw.

"Where you going with the long sack?" his father asked warmly.

There was only one place Bubber ever went with a sack, but he answered patiently. "I'm going up Kite Hill one last time," he said.

"What goes on up there?" asked Bubber's father. "What are you always going up there for?"

"A lot of things," said Bubber. "Clover. It's the only clover around anymore. There's nothing to eat down here."

"That's all it is?" asked Bubber's father. "Just the clover?"

"Just the clover," said Bubber.

"Well, why don't you get a big batch of it this time and we'll spread it around a little. Get Uncle Claude over, and the whole gang."

Bubber mumbled agreement and left the burrow, dragging his sack behind him.

The stretch of plain on the way to Kite Hill was usually teeming with activity: lemmings bustling for food, gossiping, fighting, or bartering seed for straw. But this morning the plain was quiet and empty. Bubber took note of the silence, and it filled him with foreboding. It wasn't the smooth silence of Kite Hill, but felt thick and green. It was the atmosphere that comes before a violent storm. What was happening in Bubber's home was no doubt taking place everywhere in burrow after burrow, deep under the ground. Bubber could almost feel the tense humming in the earth as he walked along.

He climbed Kite Hill, sack in hand. The hill was a favorite place of his. Clover was still plentiful on top, but since it was an exposed area, few lemmings ever ventured up there. Large birds frequented the hill on occasion, and they kept the lemmings away. Bubber didn't consider himself particularly brave, but he needed the hill for some reason besides clover, and the birds didn't frighten him. He had even gotten on friendly terms with a few of the crows, whom, in spite of their occasional hysteria, he found to be a thoughtful and interesting group. He even had one close friend among them, whom he called Crow. When Bubber arrived at the top of the hill, he found his friend sitting there, silently watching the empty plain below.

"Lemming," said Crow, by way of a greeting.

"Crow," said Bubber.

Crow was having some difficulty in looking at Bubber. His eye darted toward him for a second, and then went back to the plain below. "Quiet down there," he said cautiously.

"Mmmm," Bubber murmured. He randomly picked a bit of clover and began chewing on it.

"What's going on down there?" Crow asked.

"What do you mean?" said Bubber.

"There's no one around," said Crow. "Where is everyone?"

"Getting ready," said Bubber, easily.

"Getting ready?" asked Crow.

"Mmmm," said Bubber.

"Ready for what?" asked Crow.

"Well, it's our time," Bubber answered with a bit of a chuckle. "We're heading west."

"Heading west?" Crow asked.

"That's right," said Bubber.

Crow thought about heading west. He was up on most of the activities that took place on the plain, but this bit of information was news to him.

"Heading west are you?" he repeated.

"Heading west," said Bubber.

West of the plain by about half a mile were the Moorfield Cliffs, and beyond them the sea. Four thousand miles of open sea.

"Going to the cliffs are you?" Crow asked.

"Yes," Bubber answered.

"What is it, a picnic? Some sort of festival?" asked Crow.

"I don't know what to call it," Bubber answered. "It's just our time."

Crow found the answer a bit evasive. Something smelled fishy to him. "What will you do, spend the day out there?" he asked.

"No, we just pass right on through," said Bubber.

"Ah, I see," said Crow. He waited for some clarification, but none came. "You just continue on west."

"Right," said Bubber.

"Just keep right on going *past* the cliffs at Moorfield."

"Right," said Bubber again.

"Just keep going west into the ocean," said Crow.

"Something like that," said Bubber.

"Hmmmm . . ." said Crow. He thought about that for a moment, chuckled, shook his head, and scratched the ground.

Bubber opened his sack and started off, but Crow stopped him with a claw. "Hold on," he said.

"What's wrong?" said Bubber, shocked at Crow's abrupt action.

"Let's get this thing ironed out here," said Crow.

"I don't know what you mean," Bubber said.

"Something is a little cockeyed here," said Crow.

"In what way?" asked Bubber.

"Just hold on a minute," Crow said, and squinted upward, collecting his thoughts. "Let's get organized for a second here."

"I have to get clover," said Bubber, and he moved off again, but again Crow stopped him.

"Just be still for a minute," he said. Bubber reluctantly settled himself. "Now then," continued Crow, "who all is taking this trip?"

"All of us," said Bubber.

"All of who?" said Crow. "I'm not going anywhere."

"No, no," said Bubber impatiently. "All of lemmings. Just lemmings."

"So what is it?" said Crow, still dissatisfied. "You go down to the cliffs and jump into the ocean and swim around for a while and then what?"

"We don't know," said Bubber, his impatience mounting. The questioning was starting to make him uncomfortable. Up till now he had taken the trip for granted. Lemmings were doing something; he was a lemming.

"Can you swim?" asked Crow.

"I don't know, I never tried," said Bubber with attempted nonchalance.

"I see," said Crow. "Well, maybe it might be an idea to try it out first. What do you think? I mean that's a lot of *water* down there. Have you ever *seen* the ocean?"

"No, I don't get over there much," said Bubber.

"Well, go sneak over there and take a look. I mean that's a pile of *water* over there. How much time have you got? I can fly you over, you can take a look, and I'll have you back here in ten minutes."

"I don't think so," Bubber said. The idea that he would actually see the ocean had never really occurred to him; and the reality of it—the thought of there really being an ocean, an enormous expanse of bottomless water—was starting to make him a bit uncomfortable.

"Well then," said Crow, "how about taking a dip in a pond. Try it out first. There's one about three miles east. I can have you there in no time."

"No," said Bubber.

"How do you feel about water?" Crow asked. "The thought of immersion fill you with any joy?"

"Not particularly," said Bubber.

"Ever been in it up to your neck?"

"No," said Bubber. He pulled at his sack, which Crow was standing on. "I really can't talk anymore," he said. "I have to get back down and help out."

"You ever had a friend or a relative been in water?" asked Crow.

"No," said Bubber.

"Doesn't that sound a little *strange*?" asked Crow, with great intensity. "Doesn't that seem a bit *odd*?"

"Leave me alone!" Bubber shouted, whirling on him. "Mind your business!"

Crow threw his head back as if he'd been hit.

There was an embarrassed silence, and then Bubber moved off and began pulling clover and stuffing it into his sack.

"I'm sorry," said Crow.

"That's all right," said Bubber.

"I stepped over the line," Crow said.

"Forget it," said Bubber.

"It's just that I'm interested in animal behavior," said Crow. "If you keep your eyes and ears open you hear a lot of weirdness and, I don't know, I get excited sometimes. I ask a lot of questions, and I go over the line. You know how it is."

"I know how it is," said Bubber. There was a woodenness in his voice which told Crow the whole story.

"That's the end of that," Crow thought to himself, with some bitterness. He had ripped apart whatever there had been between them. There was no way to mend it. It would never be the same. Crow took a deep breath and cleared his throat. "Goodbye, Lemming," he said formally.

"Goodbye," said Bubber.

Crow flew off. "Write if you get work!" he called out over his shoulder, a last attempt to loosen things up, but he knew it wouldn't help.

11

Bubber picked away at the clover, fuming at Crow's insensitivity. Different animals had different ways of functioning. There were deep, mysterious currents in each species, and they were supposed to be respected. How dare Crow mock or even question a function of lemmings. Bubber finished picking the clover in a rage and went back down the hill in no mood to share it, or join in the mood that was building up underground among the lemmings all over the great plain.

2

At home, Bubber's parents were busily trying to decide what was going to be taken and what would be left behind, but since they weren't sure of where they were going or how long they would be there, it was no easy task.

Bubber slammed into the house and threw the bag of clover down in the middle of the floor.

"What's wrong?" asked his father.

"Crow," said Bubber. "He got me nervous. He crossed the line."

"That's what they do," said Bubber's father. "They're known for that."

"Well, he never did it before," said Bubber.

"Don't waste your time on a crow," said his father.

"I'm all hopped up," said Bubber, flopping down in a chair and trying to relax. "He got me all jumpy."

"What did he do?" asked Mr. Lemming. "What did he say?"

"Well, he kind of hinted that lemmings don't know how to swim," said Bubber hesitantly.

"He did, did he?" said Bubber's father, chuckling. He looked over to his wife and she chuckled back at him.

"Can you imagine?" said Mrs. Lemming.

"I hope you gave him what for," said Mr. Lemming.

"Well, I yelled at him," said Bubber. "But then I realized that I don't know if we can swim or not, so I got a little nervous."

"That's exactly the kind of thing you come to expect from crows," said Mr. Lemming forcefully.

"Is that something?" he asked his wife. "And at a time like today."

"It really is something," she answered adamantly. "It's just something."

"You can't talk to anyone anymore," said Mr. Lemming.

"That's what it's come to," said his wife.

"Well *my* advice, if you want my advice," said Mr. Lemming, "is to forget about crows. That's *my* advice." He turned to his daughter. "Sarah, run over to Uncle Claude's now, and tell them to get back here and share some of the bounty Bubber brought back for us."

"I'll do it," said Bubber, always happy for an excuse to get out of the house. He ran off, feeling somewhat relieved, but on the way to Uncle Claude's it occurred to him that his father hadn't said anything at all. Bubber had been made comfortable by his father's attitude, but as far as Bubber was concerned, the question of being able to swim was still wide open.

Halfway to Uncle Claude's Bubber ran into Arnold, a local tragedy. Arnold had been very strong in his youth, and had once saved the town from a marauding bobcat by killing it single-handedly. He became a hero, and for a time lived off the good wishes of the town. The years rolled by, however, and the single laurel that he was resting on finally wore out. To everyone's dismay, Arnold continued to rest on it. Arnold was frowned on by Bubber's parents, but Bubber found, as did many of his friends, that Arnold was more fun to be with than most of the other adults around.

"What's the good word?" Arnold said as Bubber approached.

"Nothing much," said Bubber. "I'm getting a little edgy about this thing today, is all."

"What thing today?" asked Arnold.

Bubber looked at Arnold in disbelief. "This *thing* today," he said. "This *business*. What we're *doing*." He described the same arc with his arm that Sarah had earlier. He waited for an answer from Arnold, but none came.

"The leap into the *sea*, Arnold."

"Oh yes, the leap," said Arnold without much interest.

"What do you think it's going to be like?" Bubber asked.

"How should I know," said Arnold, looking over at Bubber with genuine disinterest.

"You mean you haven't thought about it?" asked Bubber, somewhat in awe.

"No," said Arnold, radiating peace, calm and disdain.

"I don't know how you do it," said Bubber and he sat down next to Arnold and tried to radiate peace, calm and disdain. He threw out his stomach and glazed his eyes, but he still felt jumpy. "How do you do it, Arnold?" he asked.

"I don't know," said Arnold. "You just kind of go along with things as they happen."

"That's not easy to do," said Bubber.

"Well, it's the only way to travel," said Arnold.

"You're right," said Bubber, "and I try to live that way. When I woke up this morning I even forgot what was going to happen. But I went up Kite Hill and talked to this dumb crow. He asked me if lemmings could swim, and I didn't know the answer and it got me nervous."

"Oh yeah?" said Arnold, listlessly.

"Yeah," said Bubber. "And the thing is, if you want to know the truth, I don't think we *can* swim. I don't think *I* can anyway."

Arnold gazed off into the distance for a long while, then turned slowly to Bubber. "How do you *know* you can't swim?" he asked finally.

Bubber dwelled on that for a moment. "I

don't know how I know," he said. "I just never *did* it. I never saw a lemming swim. I never heard anyone even talk about swimming."

"So what does that prove?" asked Arnold in a superior manner.

"What does what prove?" asked Bubber.

"What does it prove? What does it prove?" Arnold repeated, getting a little surly. "So you never saw a lemming swim. Maybe nobody ever felt like it before."

"So how come we're doing it now?" asked Bubber.

"Maybe we feel like it now," said Arnold, easily winning the point.

"So you think we can swim?" asked Bubber hopefully.

"I didn't say that," said Arnold.

"You just said maybe we feel like it now," said Bubber.

"Maybe we do and maybe we don't," said Arnold.

Bubber nodded. "I never looked at it that way before," he said.

"The only thing I know is why the hell would anybody jump into the ocean if they can't swim?" Arnold said with great authority. "And another is that you shouldn't cross bridges until you come to them."

"Well, that's true enough," said Bubber. "But then there's 'Look before you leap.'"

"You could say that," said Arnold. His eyes glazed over as he tried to figure out some way of getting out of the discussion. He tapped Bubber on the arm, leaned over, and in a conspiratorial tone said, "Listen, what the hell do I know." He spat an enormous distance and the subject was closed. Bubber's feelings for Arnold immediately curdled. He looked long and hard at his friend, and a suspicion crossed his mind. It was that Arnold was an idiot, and that the easy confidence he had admired was really nothing but sloth. To Bubber's surprise, instead of feeling guilty, he felt liberated.

Bubber got up and stretched. "See you, Arnold," he said.

"See you," said Arnold.

3

Bubber ran off to Uncle Claude's and found when he got there the same confusion that was taking place at his own house. His cousins Floyd and Marco were fighting over an egg, his Aunt Mattie was weeping quietly, and Uncle Claude was making an angry speech about this being a time for unity and selflessness. When Bubber gave the invitation, they all seemed relieved at the idea of having something concrete to do, and immediately started back with Bubber.

"Feeling all right?" said Uncle Claude to Bubber as they walked. He slammed Bubber on the back. "You look a little green around the gills."

"I don't know how I feel, to tell you the truth," said Bubber.

"Well you'd better get yourself together,"

said Uncle Claude. "This is no time for indulgences."

"Well that's the problem," said Bubber, trying to keep up with the swift pace set by his uncle. "I'm not sure what's going on."

"In what sense," said Claude.

"In the sense that I don't know what's going on today," said Bubber.

"We're heading west, stupid," said Cousin Floyd. "Don't you know we're heading west?"

"Watch that mouth," said Claude sharply to his son.

Bubber stopped short and turned to the group. "What is this west business?" he asked. "Everyone's talking about going west. But what it *is* is that we're jumping into the ocean. The cliffs at Moorfield go straight down, there's no beach at all, we don't know how to swim, so what's going on here?"

Uncle Claude stopped in his tracks, whipped Bubber around, and stared at him fiercely. "You'd better pull yourself together, Bubber," said Claude.

"Yeah, pull yourself together," said Marco.

"*I'm* speaking here," said Claude, turning on his son.

21

"Sorry," said Marco, knowing when to back off.

"Run on ahead," Claude said to his family. "Bubber and I are having a man-to-man. We'll catch up with you." He watched as his family grudgingly moved off.

When they had gone he pointed to the ground. "Sit down, son," he said to Bubber. Bubber sat. Claude slowly squatted on his haunches. "These are big doings today, son," he said. "This is the real thing. So don't make trouble. It will only spoil things for everyone."

"I think I'm going crazy," said Bubber.

"Nonsense," said Claude. "You're just asking a lot of dumb questions. Leave yourself alone."

"I don't know what's going on," said Bubber. He grabbed his uncle hard with both paws and hung on.

Claude pulled himself away. "Keep your paws off me," he said, ruffled. "That won't help. That's crazy stuff."

"I'm sorry," said Bubber, trying to control himself. "I don't know what's going on here."

"Just calm down and I'll straighten you out," said Claude, and he waited for Bubber to settle.

22

"Just grab ahold of yourself."

"I'll try," said Bubber, and he sat hunched and tense.

"Well then," said Claude, and he gathered himself for the effort, "here's the situation. We are lemmings. We are mammals, and we are animals. Let's face it. Like all animals we have our little foibles. Various animals have their various idiosyncrasies. This one does this strange thing, the other one does something else, et cetera, and so forth. And the whole thing in a nutshell is that lemmings get together every once in a while and leap into the drink. That's our little peculiarity. You follow me?" He paused, waiting for some kind of sign from Bubber, but Bubber said nothing. Uncle Claude continued. "The problem with a deal like this is that you can't take it personally. It's what we do, it's who we are, and that's that. If you start getting morose about it you just spoil it for everyone. Don't make a big thing out of it."

"Can lemmings swim?" Bubber blurted out.

"That's a good question," said Claude. "Actually, no one knows whether we can swim or not. But the hope is that we can. After all, there's about four million of us. I don't think

we'd all just jump into the drink if we couldn't swim." He waited again for a sign from Bubber. None came. "Anyway," he continued, "the way I see it, the jump is only the first step."

"What's the second step?" asked Bubber without too much hope.

"West!" said Uncle Claude, and he pointed dramatically in the wrong direction. "The second step is west!"

"When does it happen?" Bubber asked.

"When does what happen?" asked Claude, who was so caught up in his oratory that he forgot what he was talking about.

"This leap. This business," said Bubber.

"Sometime this afternoon."

"What time?"

"No one knows the exact time."

"Then how do we know when we're supposed to do it?"

"No one knows that either. It's just supposed to become clear at a given moment that it's time for the leap," said Claude. He sighed a long sigh and tapped his foot on the ground, waiting for Bubber to pull himself together. He had nothing more to say. After a while Bubber got to his feet and began walking slowly towards home. Uncle Claude followed.

The plain was still deserted. A solitary lemming popped out of a burrow, dashed a short distance, and then disappeared into another hole. The lone figure only intensified the strange loneliness of the plain on this day. It gave Bubber a chill and he shuddered involuntarily.

"Nobody's around," he said.

"Mmmm," said Uncle Claude.

"Doesn't that seem weird to you?" Bubber asked.

Claude stopped walking and for the first time noticed that the plain was indeed deserted. "I knew something was odd," he said.

"Isn't it weird?" asked Bubber.

"I don't know," said Claude. He stood drinking in the unfamiliar silence. "Actually it's kind of nice," he said. "Peaceful."

Bubber searched his uncle's face for a crack in the wall, a hint of humor, a trace of anxiety, something, but his face was a mask. "Can we swim?" he asked weakly. "Have we been able to swim right along? Is that the joke?"

"There's no joke, son," said Claude. "There just isn't any joke at all." He looked long and hard at his nephew and found himself feeling great pity for this misfit relative. He remembered back to his own time of questioning. Like the rest of his kind, he had outgrown it, and had settled finally into a wistful acceptance of himself and the condition of his people. It hadn't exactly filled him with any peace or joy, but there were other things in life. A feeling of solidarity with his kind, a tenuous belief in the future, and a semblance of order. Seeing Bubber's confusion, panic and isolation, he was sure now that his path was the right one.

Bubber returned his uncle's stare, and what he saw was something old, lost and worn-out: no longer a relative nor anything else that he could communicate with. He turned and ran off.

4

Bubber found himself running up Kite Hill, screaming for Crow at the top of his lungs. Over and over, he cried out for the big, black bird. When he reached the top he found it deserted, but a nearby jay, hearing Bubber's cries, flew off and began circling the hill in a widening spiral. Before long he had located Crow and brought him back to Kite Hill, where Bubber was still calling out for his friend.

"What is it?" Crow shrieked, flapping his wings wildly, all caught up in Bubber's hysteria.

"Take me to the pond!" Bubber demanded.

"Climb on!" said Crow, and bent low so that Bubber could grab hold. Without effort Crow soared high into the sky, the inquisitive jay following close behind.

It was Bubber's first flight, and he was terrified. Terrified of Crow's beating wings, the swift currents of air whistling in his ears, and worst of all, the moment when he dared to open his eyes and saw all of eternity between him and green earth.

Within minutes, they were inland at the pond that Crow had spoken of earlier.

"There it is below," said Crow, shouting over his shoulder.

Bubber cautiously opened one eye, and looked down at the small body of water. "Nothing to be afraid of," he thought, hanging on for dear life.

Crow landed in a diving arc, and Bubber shakily got down. In front of him was the first body of water he had ever seen. It was a pond fed by a small stream. It was quite still, and shone like black glass. Bubber slowly sat himself down, and stared long and hard at the water.

"That's the pond," said Crow. He folded his wings behind him and stood silently, waiting for Bubber to do what he had to do. Crow badly wanted to talk, to explore Bubber's emotional state, and to be of service, but he carefully restrained himself so that the morning's episode was not repeated. The jay politely flew off, and stationed himself on a rise fifty yards away.

Bubber took a deep breath, and inched forward. He sniffed at the edge, trying to get a sense of the water's identity, but nothing about it seemed familiar. Nothing in him felt called upon to explore further.

Crow cleared his throat. "If there's anything I can do, just let me know," he said quietly. "I'll be just over here." Crow turned away, and pretended to doze off, in order to give Bubber a sense of privacy.

"You'd better stay close," said Bubber. "I'm a little out of my element."

"Whatever you say," Crow said, and turned back.

Bubber lay face down on the sand, and grabbed on to a stone. Then he stretched him-

self out to his limit, and slowly immersed one toe. He left his toe in the water for a minute, and then slowly put the whole foot in. Then he did the same thing with the other foot. Then very cautiously he stood up. He turned himself around gently, and eased himself forward in the water until he was standing ankle deep. He waited for the initial shock of coldness to leave so he could better evaluate his feelings. The coldness diminished after a while, but his discomfort remained.

"That's it," he said. "I go no further."

"I'd wait a bit longer," said Crow easily. "You have to give it a chance."

"No, this is it. This is my limit," said Bubber, checking out all of his responses.

"Best be sure," said Crow, quietly.

"I'm sure," said Bubber. "I don't want any part of this. It's not me."

"It's a new experience," said Crow. "It always takes time. Think about something else."

"Like what?" asked Bubber.

"Well, I don't know," said Crow. "Think about clouds, clover, anything."

Bubber tried to put his mind onto something else, but try as he might, his attention was riveted on the cold wetness of his feet.

"No good," he said. "I'm paralyzed here."

"You want me to push you in?" said Crow.

"I don't think so," said Bubber. He was in a crouch.

"I could drop you down in the middle of the pond," said Crow eagerly.

"I don't think so," said Bubber.

"If you don't come up, I'll dive down and get you," said Crow.

"Thanks anyway," said Bubber.

"It would ease your mind if you could muster the courage," Crow said.

"I think I found out what I wanted to know," said Bubber. "Could you just get me back on land? I seem to be unable to move."

Crow flapped over to Bubber, took him by the scruff of the neck, and flew the few feet back to the beach. He placed Bubber gently on the sand. Bubber slowly came out of his crouch. He smiled at Crow. "Well, I think that takes care of being able to swim," he said. "So much for heading west."

"What do you want to do now?" Crow asked.

"I don't know," said Bubber.

"Do you want to go back, stay here, what?" Crow asked.

"I don't care," said Bubber.

"Well, I can't leave you here," said Crow. "Unfamiliar territory. You'll be worse off here than on the plain. I'd at least go back to my own turf if I were you."

"Whatever you say," Bubber replied. His sense of doom was now so complete that even his fear of flying had left him.

Crow bent down, and Bubber climbed on. The way back was much easier for Bubber, and he even began to enjoy the sensation of flight, and imagined for a while that he was somehow merged with Crow—that he was part of this free, black, soaring creature—and the thought made him happy. "It would be nice to have wings," Bubber mused. He watched the changing landscape below, and wondered how in this perfection, this green and open peacefulness, there could be such things as hunger, such things as killing, such things as disease, such things as lemmings.

When they reached familiar terrain, Bubber started to feel uneasy again. "Let me down here," he called out to Crow, not ready yet to face family.

They were at a place just west of Kite Hill. A place of fallen rock, barren of vegetation, and uninhabited by lemmings, but Bubber wanted to be alone for a while. Crow circled downward in a deep curve and landed on a slab of granite. Bubber got down. "Thank you, Crow," he said simply.

Crow wordlessly extended a wing, but Bubber chose to embrace him. They held on for a brief moment, and then stood looking at each other.

"Well," said Crow, looking for a way of summing up, but for a change the silence seemed more comfortable. He touched Bubber briefly on the face, and flew off. Bubber followed him with his eyes until Crow was out of sight.

5

The sun beat heavily on the rocks, drying out the air and making everything shimmer. It was uncomfortably hot for Bubber, but it took his mind off the confusion of the morning. The glare made it difficult to see, but that was all right too. Bubber sighed, sat down, and leaned back on his elbows, feeling no desire to return home, nor for anything else that he could name. The heat pushed at him, tried to drive him through the rocks, and Bubber wished for it to happen.

As he lay there he began to make out the sound of chopping. It was coming from a deep hole, off to one side of the slab he was on. He rose to see what it was, and when he got to the edge of the hole he could see an old lemming at the bottom of the excavation, talking to himself a mile a minute. Bubber's shadow crossed the wall of the hole, and the old lemming looked up.

"I love rocks," he said joyfully. "Can't get enough of 'em. I love the feel of 'em. *Texture!* Crazy about texture. I love the way they stratify. I love the veins of color running through them. An unexpected soft spot, a sudden metallic glitter. What do you think about that?" he asked brightly, the sweat pouring from him.

"That's nice," said Bubber.

"I couldn't care a fig about the so-called precious stuff," said the old lemming. "It's all precious to me. Every damn bit of it. I'm in this as a learning experience, pure and simple."

The old lemming scrambled up the side of his hole and found a spot of shade. "Sun," he said, pointing. "Gotta take a break. It can cook your brains out, you start talking like an idiot." He wiped his face with an old rag, and looked inquisitively at Bubber. "What are you doing here, anyway?" he asked. "Never saw another lemming out here. I never see *anything* out here except snakes. Now, I'll tell you this much. I hate snakes. I have no respect for them. They are truly loathsome creatures, and I'm speaking objectively now. They are terrible things. But I'll be honest with you. I prefer a snake to a lemming, and that's coming from a lemming. What do you think about that?"

"I think I kind of agree with you," said Bubber, smiling at the old fellow in spite of himself.

"Nonsense," said the old lemming. "You're too young to be disillusioned. You don't know pate from posterior. You're still wet behind the ears."

"I know a couple of things," said Bubber.

"You don't know about lemmings," said the old fellow. "I can give you an earful about lemmings. The universe is rife with patterns. Patterns, patterns. Everywhere you look. Down here in the rocks. The stars in the sky. Take a look at an ant colony. Take a gander at a snowflake. Organized and beautiful. Clear and simple in its purpose. But there is no pattern in the lemming. No discernible pattern of any shape, manner or form. What do you think about that?"

"Well, to tell you the truth," said Bubber, warming up to the old codger, "I think I feel the same way. I always used to think that it was me. That something was wrong with me, but I'm beginning to think that it's lemmings."

"You've got it," said the old lemming. "Lemmings are random creatures. They run amok."

"That's been my feeling," said Bubber.

"They are random," repeated the old lemming. "Like chickens. Chickens are also random."

"I've often felt that," said Bubber.

"The universe is a fine thing," said the old fellow. "The whole thing is perfect, with the possible exception of chickens and lemmings."

"What do you think of this leaping business?" Bubber blurted out, thinking that this unique individual might be able to help him in his dilemma.

"You mean the great wet walk?" asked the old fellow disparagingly.

"Yes," said Bubber.

"It's a lot of hogwash!"

"I don't get you," said Bubber.

"I mean it's a load of bushwah!"

"Bushway?" asked Bubber.

"Coo-coo berry soup," said the old lemming. "There won't be any leap."

"How do you know?" asked Bubber.

"I know my lemmings. That's how I know," said the old lemming. "What's your view?"

"I think it will happen," said Bubber.

"What have you got to go on?" asked the old lemming.

"I feel it," said Bubber.

"Not good enough," said the old lemming.

"I've been told," said Bubber. "By my father. By my mother. My uncle. Everyone knows about it. You should see what's happening down there. They're all going crazy."

"Have you ever seen a lemming act sensibly before?" asked the old lemming.

"Well, not really," said Bubber.

"So what makes this time so special?" the old lemming asked.

"I don't know," said Bubber, a bit muddled by the question. "They have so much *conviction*. They're all so convinced. So fervent."

"The whole bunch?" asked the old lemming, unruffled.

"Yes," said Bubber.

"What if your father was the only one talking about the leap? Would you believe him?"

"I guess not," said Bubber.

"Or your mother. What if it was only her?"

"I don't think so," said Bubber.

"What if it was the two of them, and only a couple of others?"

"I guess I'd have some doubt," said Bubber.

"In other words, the more lemmings you hear something from, the more true it is?"

"I think so," said Bubber.

"What if I told you to eat rocks? Would you do it?"

"Of course not," said Bubber.

"What if your mother and father and me and four other lemmings told you to eat rocks?"

"I wouldn't do it."

"Why not?"

"They're indigestible."

"How do you know?"

Bubber was starting to get annoyed. "You can tell by looking at them," he said.

The old lemming picked up a rock and looked at it. "What's wrong with this?" he asked. "It looks very appetizing to me."

"It's too big, for one thing," said Bubber.

"I can cut it up for you," said the old lemming. "Grind it down. Make a soup out of it."

"I don't know what you're getting at," said Bubber.

"I'll tell you what I'm getting at," said the old lemming. "What I'm getting at is that lemmings are crazy to begin with. Now you come and tell me that these insane creatures are acting abnormally. So what am I supposed to think? That the loonies are now rational because they've found a new way to express their insanity? Is that what you're saying?"

"I didn't think of it that way," said Bubber.

"No, you didn't," said the old lemming, getting angrier than the conversation seemed to warrant. "You didn't think like *you*. You thought like a lemming. You let three loonies make up your mind."

"It's not just three loonies," Bubber protested.

"It's *everyone*. You should see the plain. There's not a soul around. Not one lemming anywhere. They're all underground. Packing."

"*Packing!*" said the old lemming, incredulous. "What do you take along for a mass suicide?"

"It's not thought of as suicide," protested Bubber.

"But they're all in this thing together?" asked the old lemming.

"It looks that way," said Bubber.

"I doubt it."

"Why?"

"Use your head, son," said the old lemming. "When did you ever see three lemmings agree on anything? You ever sit in on a group discussion? It's chaos. Chaos! You couldn't get an agreement on what time to have lunch, never mind a mass suicide."

"Look, don't blame this on me," said Bubber. "It's been in the air ever since I can remember. It's been in the back of everyone's mind for generations. My father's father told him about it. What am I supposed to think?"

"Don't know, don't care," said the old lemming. "All I know is that if I'm going to commit suicide I'll do it when I damn well please, and not when someone blows a whistle. No one tells me what to do, or when to do it."

"Not everyone is as strong as you are," said Bubber.

"I wasn't born this way," said the old lemming. "I had to beat it into myself. It took years of diligent work. And you can't let go for a minute either. You often catch yourself sleeping on the job."

His eyes suddenly turned softer, and he sat back. He looked down at his paws, rubbing them slowly together, and started to speak again, this time almost as an apology. "Listen," he said, "we're all a little bit crazy, let's face it. But it's no good giving in to it. We can't sit back and accept it. We have to live in the hope that sooner or later the race will stabilize. We have to put ourselves into the forge and come out iron, so that when the loonies die off, we're still around to elevate the species. This is what you and I must work for." The old lemming sat back, spent from the energy he had expended. Bubber remained motionless.

"Do you see what I am saying?" the old lemming asked.

"I think so," said Bubber.

"I talk too much," said the old fellow. "Lemmings talk too much."

The two of them sat in silence for a while, sharing a bond that neither understood.

"I think I'll go back home," said Bubber finally.

"Take care of yourself," said the old lemming, already back in a world of his own.

As Bubber walked away, the old lemming jumped up and called out, "Cocky Locky the sky is falling! The sky is falling!" Then he began leaping up and down and crowing like a rooster. Bubber turned and smiled, and then went home.

6

He started to enter his burrow when he was pushed aside by his father, who, taking no notice of his son, took a position to the west, and stood motionless as a statue. Bubber watched him from the ground where he had been thrown, shocked because there was an understanding among lemmings that, for purposes of survival, entering a burrow always took precedence over leaving. His father had broken the code. Bubber was about to say something to that effect when his mother emerged from the entrance hole. As if in a trance, she pulled herself out and positioned herself next to her mate, facing in the same direction. Bubber, confused by their behavior, was about to say something when he noticed that all over the plain, in great waves, the same thing was happening. A head would emerge, two heads, and then with a rigid single motion, the

lemmings were positioned towards the west. A few seconds would go by and then a few more heads would emerge and go through the same thing. Time stopped for Bubber. All he was conscious of was this slow and developing wave of lemmings. The plain was becoming bumpy and mottled with lemmings all standing motionless and facing west; the green areas of land slowly turning mauve, then tan then brown and grey and soon the entire plain was a vast army of lemmings, all silent, motionless and facing west.

Bubber watched in horror. There was nothing

familiar about these animals. They were listen-
ing to a voice that Bubber could not hear. There
was the same precise intentness on each lemming
face. Half-closed eyes and necks craning forward, bodies leaning as if in a wind. Now the
last lemming was out of his burrow. The
children were there, the aged, the sick; and for
the first time in their short history they were
a single-purposed unity. For a long moment
they stood there, so still that they could have
been stones embedded in the earth, and then at
some unheard signal, in one body they began to
move. Slowly, very slowly the lemmings began

their trek towards Moorfield, and the cliffs. As
the march got under way, the pace quickened.
The younger lemmings moved toward the front,
the older ones to the rear, and yet, with all the
variety of step and pace, they remained one
organism. There was only one thought.

Fearful of what lay ahead, but even more
afraid of complete isolation, Bubber threw himself into the crowd. It was defeat, and Bubber
knew it, but it was mixed with great relief. All
decisions were gone. So was concern for the future, so was the fear of conflicting with his own
kind.

He darted this way and that, and before long caught up with his father. Bubber smiled at him as if to say, "Look, I have joined with you. We are together now." But his father's eyes had become dead weights in his head. He did not recognize his son. Bubber walked with his father, trotted with him, and when the trot became a run, he ran with him.

The only sound audible now was the padding of a million tiny feet. On and on they ran, and before long the gait had steadied and they were running in unison. All of them, old and young, firm or soft, were running as they had never run before. The eyes which had been half-closed were now glazed and staring blankly ahead toward an unseen horizon. Their breathing came in long gasps now, as their lungs burst with the need for more oxygen. For the first time in his life Bubber felt close to his people. He ran and ran, straining and panting, holding pace with his father, his feet falling into rhythm with a million other feet. To the left, in the distance, he saw his sister and called out to her, but she didn't hear him. His mother was nowhere to be seen.

In the distance now, over the sound of the million padding feet, came the low, soft sighing of the ocean. It was calling gently to the tiny

army, and its sound was lulling and pleasant. Its whisper spoke of ancient secrets and the completion that each lemming yearned for.

A sigh ran through the ranks of lemmings, and with the sound of the goal in their ears, they summoned up new energy. Their pattern now shifted; the most desperate of them moved forward, becoming the leaders, bursting lungs and muscles in an attempt to complete themselves and join their destiny.

Bubber was one with his people. His breath

was a whistle now, coming so regularly that its rhythm was the drumbeat that spurred him on. It was his only awareness. As he scrambled up the huge rock pilings, he passed the old lemming, but they were beyond recognizing each other. The old lemming had tried to stem the tide. He had stood waving his arms at the multitudes, cursing at them, and demanding a return to reason, but they were beyond hearing and squashed him like a bug. Half-conscious, he was now being helped to his fate by the tide of lemmings behind him, pushing him, shoving him, till he turned over and over, bouncing this way and that, a cork in another sea. He would make it over the edge the way the rest of the elderly and lame would make it. By being washed in by the sea of lemmings behind. Over the crest of the rocks now, the leaders could see the ocean for the first time. The vast expanse of it came up all at once, and its sighing, yearning call turned into a roar. Had they been possessed of their senses, its vastness and beauty would have stopped them, at least for a moment, but they were robots now, and unstoppable.

Over the side they leaped and fell. A brown and grey cascade. Flowing gracefully in a long slow wave, nothing animal remaining, nothing

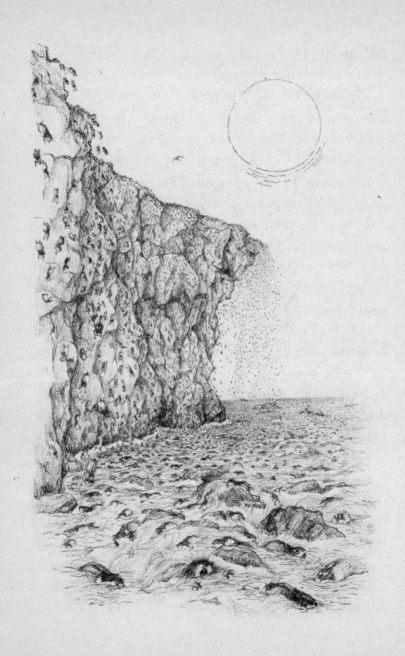

of intelligence, they were now a long dark waterfall dropping gently to the sea.

Bubber reached the top of the bluff, and saw the ocean. Something in him stopped as if he had been hit. But he was pushed onward by the tide behind him. He could begin to make out the huge rocks below him, and he could see thousands of lemmings spewing from the cliffs and falling onto the great jumble of stone below, bouncing this way and that, and then disappearing into the cauldron of the sea.

Something deep in Bubber called out to him, and he was filled with fear. He saw in an instant the horror taking place all around him, and he screamed. He tried to stop himself, but the wave of lemmings pushed him forward. He fought to turn himself around, but there was no room. He twisted and clawed and bit at the mass of bodies around him, but they paid no mind. They were pushing him onward. Bubber now began to sense his exhaustion. His eyes were choked with dust and his lungs were on fire, but he tried with all his might to fight and claw his way back from the edge of the cliff; tumbling head over heels, now being stepped on, now being pushed and shoved, screaming all the way, he managed

to keep from going over. A stone gave way, and
he slipped into a small crevice between two
rocks. It was not deep enough to hide him, but
it allowed him to brace himself against the tide.
He pushed himself into the furrow and threw
his arms over his head while the lemming army
ran on, climbing over him and everything else
in their way. For an eternity he hung on, crying
with pain and exhaustion. Through the whole
first wave of lemmings, Bubber continued to
hang on. He hung on through the second,
smaller wave. He hung on while the stragglers
and maimed crawled ecstatically over the edge,
and in the silence following, he also hung on.
Even when sleep came, with its oblivion, he
continued to hang on.

On the following morning the sun rose
slowly, hesitantly, as if it were ashamed to
witness what had taken place. Its rays crept over
the barren plain, searching for life. It flowed
slowly over the rocky face of the cliffs, with
fingers that reached into cracks and crevices,
and found Bubber, warmed him, and brought
him back to life. It comforted and nourished

him. It spoke to him and caressed him, and by midmorning Bubber was able to raise himself and survey what had happened.

Carefully and painfully he stood up and walked away from the cliffs. As he looked around he felt things being pulled away from him. Emptying him out. He was out of breath and slightly euphoric. He started crossing the great plain which had been his home for all of his life, and the home of all lemmings. Nothing was left but an empty, trampled expanse of field. Dust and bits of grass blew in the wind, telling of the great activity that had taken place there. It was a graveyard. A place of death. Bubber stood silently watching the dust rise. He looked at the shambles of what had been his life, the life of all lemmings, and he felt no emotion at all. It was burned right out of him.

As he stood there he saw a small head emerge from the ground. It was a dazed and confused baby lemming surveying the world. Further away another head emerged, then another. Before long five young lemmings had emerged from their burrows. They closed the space between them and began sniffing around, trying to determine what had happened.

"This is the future," thought Bubber. "This

is how we've survived. These few will rebuild the whole civilization, and in a few generations the whole business will happen all over again."

Bubber took a deep breath and began walking. He passed the young lemmings, who were already looking for bits of seed and cleaning out their burrows.

"Did you see it?" one called out to him on his way by.

"I did," said Bubber.

"I guess we missed the whole thing!" said one, laughing.

"I stayed up, and stayed up, and then slept right through it!" said another.

They had slept through the moment that made their species unique, but they would talk about that moment for their entire lives. Their children would talk about it, and in time would begin to yearn for it. Bubber walked on past the young lemmings, and started east, inland, away from the sea.

"Where are you going?" one of the young ones called out.

"I don't know," said Bubber.

"Can't you help us with this? There's an awful lot to do," another said.

"No," said Bubber. He kept going.

"You *have* to help!" one called to him. "We all have to help each other."

"*You* help each other," Bubber said. "I'm not one of you."

"Yes you are!" they shouted. "You are a *lemming*. You *are* one of us."

"Not anymore," said Bubber. "I'm not a lemming anymore."

"What are you then?" they called.

"I'll let you know when I find out," said Bubber. He pointed himself true east and was on his way.